Merry Christmas,
MARY & LUCY !
Love, Gipper
2009

A PHOTOGRAPHIC FANTASY

Lost *in the* Woods

Carl R. Sams II & Jean Stoick

Acknowledgements

We would like to thank our loyal staff: Karen McDiarmid, Becky Ferguson,
Bruce Montagne, Margaret and Tom Parmenter, Jennifer Bush, Dawn Clements
and Mark Halsey for their contributions in the creation of this book;
Carol Henson for editing;
Laura Sams, Rob Sams and Douglas Peterson for their creative suggestions;

Greg Dunn, Mark Hoppstock, Deb Halsey, Tyler Evert and Heiner Hertling for their artistic contributions;
Rob Mies, Kim Williams and their daughters, Georgia Sky and Madison Autumn,
for their ideas and patience;
Danny, Sue and Nancy Boyd for suggestions and video contributions.

Special thanks to K Halpin Weston and Rick and Carol Bearss. Without their help this book
would not have been possible. K Weston is an angel sent to care
for our wild creatures. She is truly an inspiration.

Carl R. Sams II Photography, Inc.

2675 General Motors Rd.
Milford, MI 48380
800/552-1867 248/685-2422 Fax 248/685-1643
www.lostinthewoods.biz   www.strangerinthewoods.com   www.carlsams.com

Karen McDiarmid — Art Director

Sams, Carl R.
Lost in the Woods: A Photographic Fantasy
by Carl R. Sams II & Jean Stoick, Milford, MI
Carl R. Sams II Photography, Inc. © 2004

Summary: A spring tale of trust, patience, and
waiting for your time. Woodland creatures are
concerned for a newborn white-tailed fawn they believe is lost.

Printed and bound in Canada
Friesens of Altona, Manitoba

ISBN 0-9671748-8-0

Fawn (white-tailed deer) /Nature/Spring
- for children of all ages.

Library of Congress Control Number: 2004092476

10 9 8 7 6 5 4 3 2 1

For those who
protect wild places
and care for
wild things.

The spring frogs sing-singing with a thousand trilling

voices were silenced by the rising sun.

New life came to the woods
    before the sun touched the tops of the trees.

He slept quietly in the tall grass
        on the north edge of the meadow
    where the trees start the forest.

"Get up!
Get up!
Get up!"
shouted the
red-winged blackbird.

"Shhh . . .
    shhh,"
        hushed the mouse.

"I think he's lost.
Just let him sleep."

"I've been watching you.
You've been alone
for a long time,"
said the chipmunk,
stuffing another acorn
into his fat cheeks.

"I hear you're lost."

"Mama said to wait,
to wait right here," whispered the fawn.
"She will come back."

"Ahh-hah!
    So you're the
              lost babe
        in the woods,"
announced the cardinal.

"I'll use my red-red color
and fly through the treetops,
        signaling for help."

"I'm not lost,"
        said the fawn,
not looking up at all.
    "She will come.
            She said she would."

The sun climbed to a higher place in the sky,
drying out the morning dew.

The fawn stood alone in the tall, shadowed woods.

Stretch your legs to make them strong,
but don't wander too far.

"Where did he come from?"
"Should he be here?"
The goslings jabbered
all at the same time.
"Where is his mother?"
"His ears are so-ooo big!"
"Is he dangerous?"

"Where is-sss
your mama?"
hissed Mother Goose.

"She said she'd be back . . .
she will,"
called out the startled fawn,
turning toward the woods
that seemed larger
and lonelier than before.

Did I go too far?

The sound of
loud voices and laughter
carried on the wind.

The birds suddenly
stopped singing.

The fawn dropped
down to hide in
the tall grass.

When trouble comes looking for you,
          lie still, oooh so very still.

          Don't blink an eye.
                    Don't twitch an ear.
                              Let your spots work,
          and don't make a sound.

You are a newborn,
          born without a scent.
          Trouble's nose will not find you.

"Well done,"
chirped a voice
    from nowhere.

    "I can hear you,"
        said the fawn,
        "but I don't see you."

    "That's because I'm the
master of camouflage,"
        boasted the tree frog.
"Green is my color.
I find my color
        and I'm out of sight!"

"Look how he used his spots.
He did. He did," said Katydid,
looking down from her leaf.
"Mother Doe would be
so pleased."

"Tut-tut-tut!" chattered the squirrel.
"Do you suppose Spotty's hungry?

Tut-tut-tut! Not to worry. . . not to worry.
I've tucked them here.
I've tucked them there.
Hundreds of acorns. Sea-sons ago.

And did I not tell you . . . I doo-oo share.
Most defi-NUT-ly!"

"Oooh yes,"
flapped the dragonfly.
"I'll zoom-zoom
through the meadow
as fast as my wings can fly.
I will bring back food!"

"Good idea," said the turtle.
"I'll just wait
right here."

"Who-hoo-hoo
do I see?"
hooted the little
saw-whet owl.
"Someone's moving through
my woods.
I saw-whet!
I saw-whet!"

"Who's coming
through the woods?
Where?"
bleated the fawn.

Suddenly . . .
a shadow darkened
the warm sun.

The fawn turned
to look into the
dark brown eyes
of his mother.

"I knew you would come."

"Remember this," she said,
licking his spotted
coat smooth.
He lifted his ears
to listen to mama's
words once more.

"You are a newborn
born without
a scent . . .

I have to leave
        so trouble's nose
cannot find you.
                Stretch your legs, make them strong,
                but don't go far.
        Soon it will be your time,
                your time to follow me."

Her words
were remembered,
as he drifted
off to sleep.

The sun chased away the night
as it had done
many times before.

The meadowlark sang
his morning song.

Days passed by and
the fawn grew stronger
as did the other
babes in the woods.

"I can,
    I know I can!"
        puffed the determined raccoon,
struggling to keep from falling off the log.

"I . . . I can do-oo it!"

"What are you doing?"
asked the fawn.

"Climbing trees.
I'm getting good at it, too,"
bragged the little raccoon.
"Do you climb trees?"

"I don't think I can climb trees,"
answered the fawn.
"But my legs are
getting stronger."

"Tomorrow is the most important
day of my life,"
chirped the baby chickadee-dee-dee.
"Tomorrow I'm fledging!

"You are what?"
asked the fawn,
wrinkling
his nose.

"Fledging!
I am going to flutter my wings and fly.
I need to work out a few wobbles,
then I'll fly up there with the big birds.
A great, great day indeed!

When do you fledge?"

"I don't know if I can fly," said the puzzled fawn,
"but I think my time is near."

"Could it be?
    Is . . . is it his time?"
sputtered the
raccoon from above.

Up popped the goslings.

"Say what?"
        "Say what?"
    "Say what?"

"It's time!   It's time!"
shrieked the
red-winged blackbird.

"Ready?" asked Mother Doe. "There's so much to see!"

"Yes . . . it's time. I'm ready!"

The End

*I knew
he wasn't
lost.*

Tiger
Swallowtail

Toad

Can you turn
through the pages and
help me find my friends?
They're *Lost in the Woods!*

Grasshopper

Dragonfly

Chipmunk

Caterpillar

Cottontail Rabbit

White-footed Mouse

Thirteen-lined Ground Squirrel